TEARS AND LAUGHTER

Audrey Rodgers

Published by Kaye Productions

www.kayeproductions.com

ISBN 978-0-9829716-4-2

PRINTED IN THE UNITED STATES OF AMERICA

1 3 5 7 9 10 8 6 4 2

First Edition

Because he was my brother, because he brought fun and wisdom and affection and affirmation and love to so many, because he enriched my life, I am moved by memory to tell his story.

A humble thanks to Candy and David Kaye for their support.

Contents

Prologue................................... 1

In the Beginning 5

Coming of Age 27

Funny Man 33

Becoming A Physician......... 39

Patty 45

The Children's Hour.............. 55

After Great Pain 61

The Last Hurrah..................... 75

Alan and Audrey 83

The Worldly Hope................. 87

TEARS AND LAUGHTER

Prologue

His name was Alan and he was our wunderkind. Not that he was different from hundreds of other beautiful babies born in the Bronx in 1933. It was a matter of lineage for we were a family of girls who kept appearing throughout the generations with no hope of saving the unique name of Tropauer.

Davie, my father, bemoaned the fact that we would slip away from the chronicles of time—our lifeline lost forever! And then—miracle of miracles—my mother brought forth—after ten years, two little girls and after hours of overpowering pain—a son. Davie was wild with joy, my mother weak with exhaustion but clearly victorious in her fight against anonymity.

The name "Tropauer" was saved for yet another generation and the golden-haired infant with green eyes, a chubby pink face, and a bewitching smile would become the star of the family. And so Alan took his destined place as the Pride of the Tropauer heritage. No baby in our time received so much love, so much attention, so much promise.

Seventy-six years go by quickly.…Only yesterday I followed the procession to the grave where Alan was laid to rest. Even now, numbness overcomes me and my eyes blur with tears. Images tumble through my mind—disjointed, fragmentary, random. Alan's mop of blonde baby curls, Alan sipping cocoa with me on frosty winter mornings before school, Alan standing tall at Bellevue's Medical School graduation, Alan with his first son in his arms.

I whisper, "Alan is gone and leaves a richness and humor and vitality, but my world is diminished by his absence."

Where we go
He goes with us.

Denise Levertov

Chapter I

In the Beginning

When I was very young, I sometimes wondered how my life might have been different as an only child—lavished with attention and love. But today, the last of my siblings, I feel only the nadir of emptiness, a solitude too heavy to bear. No matter that my loving son indulges me with attention and affection—his love is of a different flavor. The somber knowledge that Elinor and Alan are gone is the inescapable fact that some part that was me is forever absent. Fighting or loving, teasing or envying, sharing or giving, we three were one.

As I look back over the years, we were a happy family. There was enough love to go round. I was my mother's "baby" until the age of ten; and Alan was the jewel in the Tropauer crown. We rarely talked of love, rarely embraced except on birthdays, and generally demonstrated little of the affection we felt for each other. My father was strict with his offspring—there were countless don'ts to be heeded, but the miracle is that we were three obedient children who secreted a mild fear of our father. Yet he never punished us, never raised a hand to us, and never made us feel inferior.

My mother, famous for her red-headed temper, kept us in line with the ominous threat: "I'll tell your father!" followed with a tempestuous outburst that reduced the three of us to panic. My father, oblivious to the characterization of a punitive warlord, happily retained the love and respect of us all. Needless to say, my mother never told my father of our minor infractions of the Tropauer ethic.

During the 30's, America was gradually but surely uplifting itself from the depths of the Depression. With the optimism of Franklin Roosevelt's vision, Americans geared up, took renewed hope in the future and turned their efforts to the dark clouds threatening on the horizon. With the pressure on the United States to furnish arms, planes, and the multitudinous apparatus demanded by World War II, jobs multiplied and the average American felt the money jingling in his pocket. Little did they envision the loss of American youth on European battlefields, and the spectacle of D-Day is still beyond the comprehension of many.

Our own family bathed in the luxury of the newly found security. Once again, patients paid my father a fee. While the War was still raging in Europe, Davie made daily house calls in new cars supplied by uncle Victor's vast auto empire.

Fulfilling a long held dream, Davie bought a strip of land in the mountains near Newburgh, New York and commissioned a local builder to construct a beautiful cabin with a view of distant hills, fields of blueberries, and a stretch of white birch trees. For years, the family escaped the

7

searing heat of the city, and the cabin became our home away from home. There were no other houses nearby. We enjoyed our solitude, the hum of the bees, and the sweetness of cool, fresh air. My

father drove up on weekends and my mother would present sumptuous meals. My most c h e r i s h e d memories recall the beauty of the awesome hills and the tart flavor of blueberries. At dusk, my father would read poetry to us until we slipped off to sleep.

My love for poetry was born in my father. For years he would quote to us from the "Rubaiyat of Omar Khayyam":

Into this Universe and Why not knowing
Nor Whence, like water, willy-nilly flowing
And out of it. As wind along the Waste
I know not Whither willy-nilly blowing.

We listened, not fully understanding the words until years later, but lulled by the lure of the sounds as my father spoke them. Today, I can still hear my father's voice intoning Fitzgerald's wisdom.. And there were others—"The Wreck of the Hesperus," Longfellow's "The Children's Hour," and "Hiawatha." As a young child, I echoed my father's love for poetry. In the mountains, I spent most of my time reading poems, picking berries, or dreaming of the year ahead. I wrote short stories and helped my mother cook or played with the "baby." Looking back—the mountains, the isolation, the silence and the beauty of the snow-white birches were the single pristine adventure of my life. Years later, when I lost my three-day old son, the soothing atmosphere in those hills served to heal my wounds.

But as Elinor and I grew older, the summer retreat lost much of its charm—we both longed for the excitement of the city, our friends, and the attraction of boys. Little by little, we opted to remain in the city with Davie and we visited the mountains on rare occasions.

A tall, blue-eyed charmer, Les, came into Elinor's life, and this first family romance consumed us all. Les was everything a beautiful, intelligent nineteen year old could dream of. He adored Elinor and in a few short months they eloped as the War loomed threateningly in the future. Before long, Les received his induction orders in the Dental Corps. He was the youngest graduate at Columbia University and the first to disperse our family to far corners of the United States. Little did we know that we could never recapture the intimacy of Davie's "Walden"...

The War became a significant part of our lives. Soon after Elinor and Les were married, they travelled to New Orleans, where Les served in the U.S. Army for the duration. The mountain retreat became a "sometimes thing" for we had changed. We were "grown-ups" in a child's fantasy. The Catskills were the past, and we were ready to leave the silence, the birch trees, and the blueberries to others.

With the world in turmoil our individual lives reflected the uncertainty of the future. No longer did we view summer as a retreat from the city; we bid "Goodbye" to men in uniform—secure they would return, yet in our inner selves fearful of the dreaded knock upon the door. How vividly I can recall the sailor I took to Barnum & Bailey's circus or the young marine to the huge amusement park in Coney Island, or the lieutenant who wanted to dance all night to the music of Tommy Dorsey at the Astor Hotel. As for our private lives, Elinor and I continued to drift apart.

As children, Elinor and I were bound together, but as we grew older, profound differences in temperament, stature, and intellectual ability estranged us. The War imposed further alienation.. We rarely spoke of this, and, despite all, acknowledged the bond of sisters.. Yet, our affinity had far-reaching contradictions. Elinor carried a burden for life, believing that she was to blame for the sexual attack on me when, in her care, I was assaulted. That tragic moment affected us all! Elinor, a mere seven years, had been charged with watching me on the open street, but I wandered off in search of my grandmother who lived nearby. Caught in the isolated building, I found that my grandmother was not home. Trapped on the lonely stairs, I was assaulted sexually by a stranger.. I ran home, screaming, to my horrified mother. I can still hear my cries of bewilderment and terror. Gently, my mother washed the semen from my quivering body and I was sworn to secrecy.

It is difficult to measure the "effect" of a violent act upon a four or five year old child. As I try to reconstruct the rape, my mind closes down, leaving an emptiness, a void, and then…the mental image of a child running through the streets screaming wildly. Still, the fragmented echo of weeping refuses to disappear and now, as an adult, it haunts me, lingering on, a shred too painful in its clarity.

The "protective" reaction is to banish it from one's mind. But that is the impossible—for the rest of my life the trauma of the event remains in my memory. For millions of people, the painful recollections are more tenacious than the blissful ones. So was the first violent act of my life!

My father was never told! For Elinor, the spectre of that traumatic day haunted her dreams. As she told me years later, her nights recreated the awful moment when she "failed". For me, the act was blotted out of my consciousness, and I had merely hazy occasional images of a secret that no one must ever know. Whether or not I was actually raped would remain a mystery for life, but the trauma would linger in dreams and in Elinor's sense of guilt. To the end of her life, my mother never mentioned a word.

It is always difficult to express sibling relationships. They are complex, often contradictory, often irrational. Such was the ever-changing state in the lives of Elinor, Alan, and me. We three Tropauer children were variations on the theme of Rosie, our grandmother, though our profound differences were not immediately apparent. True—we all had Rosie's green eyes, Rosie's round cheeks, and, most visibly, Rosie's temperament. But beneath these recognizable traits, we differed one from the other yet sharing an abundant amount of complex resentment hidden in the recesses of the mind.

I could say with some certainty that envy was the fatal flaw that threatened a "perfect" relationship between Elinor and me, between Alan and Elinor, between Alan and me. Was there also love? We would assert forcefully that we loved each other as siblings do, that we would die if need be for the other, that we would protect each other against the vagaries of the world…yet the negative element was always there. The simple truth was that—in fact—not a shred of support justified these assumptions!

Alan protested that Elinor was Davie's favorite child, that I was my mother's favorite, and that he was no one's favorite. Of course, this was sheer nonsense since the entire family doted on Alan, "punished" him with kisses and spoiled him to distraction. But perhaps the most bitter envy existed between the two sisters. It began with our physical appearance. Clearly Elinor was healthier while I was frail as a child and frankly envious of El's tall build, striking color and overall strong impression. But, more painful for me was her beauty—black, Curly hair, huge green eyes and a delicately chiseled nose. Heads turned in admiration when she walked, and I yearned to look like her. My mother added to my distress with her oft-repeated observation: "Elinor has beauty but my Audrey has charm." Needless to say, I grew to hate that word! Education was the next source of bitter envy. Elinor was a brilliant student throughout her life. As a Chemistry and Physics Major at Hunter College, she never fulfilled her potential. Her marriage and subsequent three children made it impossible to enter graduate work. Demands upon her time and the effort of a busy household postponed her studies until the children were launched on their own careers. Yet she did return to gain a Master's Degree in Chemistry and an enviable appointment in a distinguished high school. Nonetheless, this did not satisfy Elinor who cast envious looks at my own progress in higher education. Because my husband introduced me to the University world through his own studies in Geography I began a long career as an English Department Instructor at the University of Wisconsin and finally, for thirty-eight years as a professor at The Pennsylvania State University. The going was challenging but I had found my true talent and my true love. Fate had dealt me one blow. I was able to have just one child, but had I more I may not have pursued my career. Envy? Elinor never recovered from my advancement and told me once :

"People become professors because they can't succeed at anything else."

There was no question that—at least to Accademe—a Ph.D. was more prestigious than a Masters Degree, though I repeatedly told her that her intelligence far exceeded many professors I knew. But the envy was too deep-rooted to convince Elinor otherwise and publication reinforced an old myth. But this was not all. Completely unconscious

16

of her delicately beautiful looks, Elinor revered the intellect and would only consider marriage to a man superior to her in intelligence.

This did not prevent her inner tendency to envy others who had reached further ground on the academic route. My own achievement in earning the Ph.D. was a further source of envy she found it difficult to overcome. To exacerbate this further was the issue of publication.

We are all familiar with the phrase "Publish or perish." This was the mandatory understanding at Penn State and so I was engaged in the publication race. I loved both teaching and writing articles and books in my field of 20th century American poetry, although I knew it was both a source of pride and envy for my sister.

Elinor was clearly the beauty of the family. Her face was chiseled into delicate features: her large green eyes, straight small nose, and full sensuous mouth recalled her grandmother's striking beauty. The jet black curls framing her face were enhanced by her tall slim figure and her proud bearing. There was no question in our family—Elinor was truly the radiant star among us. Yet, almost indifferent to her beauty, she disdained any man who was not a dedicated student. Intelligence was all! She accepted few dates. Her temper flared easily, her pride ever discernible, her emotional quotient always high. Elinor was, at the least, difficult to live with!

The significant element in my relationship with my sister was that all our lives we wavered between dislike and love. The reasons were profound and complex, a possible result of Elinor's haunting sense of responsibility and my own feelings of inferiority. It was a given that the "older" child was the "caretaker" of the younger child. For the first time, I realized the burden she had carried much of her life. To Elinor, she had failed.

For as long as I can recall, Elinor and I were at war. Whether trivial or serious, we were like two armies reluctant to give up the fight. In short, intermittent moments there was peace, but it never lasted and we always found the opportunity to hurt each other. The intensity of our antagonism lasted; the hostility grew with each encounter.

In a letter Elinor wrote to me, one can feel the depth of her antipathy:

> …being apart most of our lives inevitably eats away at a relationship. I can't pretend that my feelings haven't changed over the long years. That does not mean I have hatred or venom. I am so neutral. I am mostly neutral and calm…

I would assert that families rarely outlive their complex feelings for each other despite many separations or crises, and my sister never was either neutral or calm! When angered, she was malicious and cold; when happy she was charming and effusive. I was told by friends that Elinor spoke proudly of my advancement at the University, of the several books I had written, of my reputation as a professor. There was love in those claims! Her denials to me were only meant to hurt. I never knew how to please her. I never knew how to compensate for the ill will she felt. I never knew how to like her.…I might add that Alan was totally neutral in these encounters, but I always sensed that he respected El more and loved me perhaps a little more.

Three years younger than Elinor, I was the "middle child" in our family. I was named for my great-grandmother, Honey, whose name I can trace on a yellowed copy of Rosie's marriage certificate. Tragically, I was born with a crippled right arm, thanks to an incompetent doctor who brought me into this world. For more than ten years I knew only doctors' offices, exercises at home, dancing to strengthen my arm, and the overwhelming protection of my mother who both loved me too much and refused me a normal life. I was small in stature, frail, and susceptible to illness as a child when my father, a physician, transmitted numerous childhood diseases to our home. I was always the first victim!

Yet, with each year and my mother's urgency, I grew stronger. I was, and still am. a Tropauer— green eyes, impish nose, curly hair but less confident than my older sister. I lacked Elinor's brains, Elinor's striking looks, and Elinor's aggressiveness. I struggled in school though

I worked hard to no avail. Still, I was a happy child with many friends and the affection of my mother. With growing confidence in myself, I found my love in poetry and literature. My grades improved. I was admitted to Hunter College...to my father's surprise. I proudly made the Dean's List in my third year. I was growing up! At twenty, my dating life was exciting.—to the amazement of my parents who thought Elinor would have been more popular. I always felt my dates were trying to protect me, perhaps because the family pointedly emphasized Elinor's looks. But when the phone rang, it was always for me.

Yet, the years before marriage—with all its changes—were happy and rewarding for me. I attended a high school for girls, studied intensely to meet Elinor's challenge, and cherished the letter accepting me to Hunter College. I soon developed a "Hunter" personality: intellectually acute, confident with an over-abundance of Hunter Chutspa....I moved in a circle of beautiful, popular, and aggressive young women. There was Bess Myerson, Elise Becker, and Lucille Porter— all destined to lead distinctive lives, but always

"Hunter Girls." My grades rose as did my faith in my ability to succeed after college. Nonetheless, I still envied Elinor, her handsome husband, and three beautiful children. Neither of us succeeded in overcoming this insidious tendency.

Without knowing that my life would change forever, I met a young Ensign in the Navy whose blue eyes and beautiful speaking voice bewitched me. He was twenty years old and his name was Allan. Despite his youth, he was sophisticated—he knew wines, French restaurants, the latest hits and the best seats on Broadway and I fell in love!

Allan's ship, a destroyer escort, came into New York every eight weeks,. and for the ten nights of Allan's leave I was introduced to New York's finest. But my Ensign was no "playboy"—he was intelligent, well-read, ambitious about the future and in love with me. Within a year, we were engaged and married. Because of the War and Allan's Naval duties, a wedding was impossible. Without a trailing white gown, a bevy of \bridesmaids, a "chuppa" of flowers, and a sumptuous feast, our humble union lasted sixty-eight years!

My earliest memory of my brother Alan was of a delicate infant who—despite his chubby face and sunny disposition—worried my mother who fought desperately to strengthen him. He was allergic to milk, to most baby food, to all manner of delicacies. Yet he thrived, and in a few months adapted to the world he had entered. Alan was precocious. He talked before he walked; he laughed when other babies whimpered; he accepted warmly the enormous attention lavished upon him. He rarely cried and was the blonde, rosy-cheeked favorite of our household. His incessant chatter gave a sweetness of fresh life to our "playtime" and the chance to be the pet of three adoring "mothers." Davie, his ultimate dream fulfilled was already planning Alan's life as a doctor, while my mother—her arms encircling her small son—whispered "Schluf mein fagela" in his ear.

He was easy to love. As he grew older and was less a pet and more a person, Alan was the bright spot in our lives. When a child, he never fought with either sister, never entered our arguments by taking sides, and generally gave each of us a wide berth when the battles were dangerously destructive. Elinor and I were beginning to think more of boys and date while Alan was still enveloped in "child's play." His bevy of friends filled our house with their youth, their laughter, their antics. They talked incessantly played games of sheer nonsense, and always seemed to be having a wonderful time!

And there were those unforgettable moments that shall live with me forever and still bring both tears and laughter to my memories. On a bright autumn afternoon, Alan was outside our windows playing ball with a friend. He was six years old, his blonde hair damp, his cheeks red and sweaty from exertion. Suddenly, he heard his father's voice, urging him to come in and wash up for supper. Standing straight, arms at his side—openly challenging—Alan shouted back:

"You're a bum and a louse and a rat!"

Then, giggling all the way, he raced into the building, knowing the punishment his father would exact. But we, all shocked by Alan's outburst, laughed at our "angel's" moment of rebellion. I think he never used those words again, but the family never forgot his moment of triumph. In the long life of a 76 year old man, why do I remember a small, tow-headed boy, arms akimbo, challenging his father.

In his own way, Alan was growing, but so imperceptibly that I was conscious merely of my own "successes"—totally unaware that this most important element of my life had left "childhood" behind. Memories are indiscriminate, elusive, often haphazard. We don't know when they will seize us; we don't know when they will please or sadden us. We cling to our memories because they bring nostalgic or heart-wrenching moments into a banal present. So the memory of a six year old, standing in open confrontation with his father, moves me to both laughter and tears. It was Alan's first leap into the arena of defiance. During the years when Elinor and I were completely inundated with both school and our growing social life. Alan, to us, was still the family "baby" entering the world of reading, writing, and making new friends. In his own way, Alan was growing, but so imperceptibly that I was conscious only of my own "successes"—

totally unaware that the "baby" was growing up and thriving in his newly-discovered world. Each day he came more to look like Davie's son—green eyes, chubby cheeks. 1 small mouth that, when smiling, tilted upward and sent a whimsical message. He was becoming—as my mother would fondly say—a mench!

Chapter II

Coming of Age

"Coming of Age" for a sheltered, inexperienced, twenty-year old still in college meant marriage in our Rabbi's study with only our parents present. There were no "guests", no flowing white wedding gown, no honeymoon. It was in every sense a War Marriage. In one whirlwind moment my life changed completely. I was still studying at Hunter, but Allan—my new husband—spent months aboard his destroyer escort. His ship returned to the States every eight weeks, and I would take the train to Boston to be with him. The entire focus of my life centered on the ten days that Allan's ship was in port, and I gave little thought to study, to my family, or to the future.

In many ways, this period was most difficult for Alan, for—since birth—he had counted on me for support and companionship. He continued to study hard and seek company with his friends, but the early camaraderie seemed gone forever. Elinor was living in New Orleans and rarely came home. Her life was with her Army husband and her small daughter. Those were lonely months for a boy at the threshold of his teens. Such changes hastened his self-sufficiency, his growing up! We used to say, "Twelve, going on forty-five!" The ten years between us seemed more like twenty, especially as the War drew to a close and Allan returned, only to hurry me off to Madison, Wisconsin and three long years of Graduate study.

I loved our life in Wisconsin—not only for the exciting experience of graduate study with some of the best minds in the country—but because Madison was beautiful, circling around three blue lakes and resplendently constructed as the capital of the state. All this meant that I was drifting further and further away from home, my former love for a large city, and—most of all—Alan.

Our trips home were infrequent, the intimacy we had enjoyed dimming as the years progressed. My talkative, mischievous, fun-loving little brother was quieter, more inward and serious, less prone to confide in me and more complex. Alan's life as a high school student was busy with study, reports, massive amounts of reading, and the small amounts of pure play with his childhood friends. Our visits were short and hurried, but I had little time to absorb Alan's progress in depth. We were still close, but there were changes. He was more a contemporary than a "kid brother" and our discussions were almost always Hemingway and Fitzgerald and the "difficulties" of physics!

But there was something fresh and new in him that I discovered—a growing sense of humor unusual in a teenager. There was a cutting edge, a subtlety, an irony in both his writing and his speech.! He "amused' but he also satirized whatever came into his sight. This remained a quality throughout his life.

Even in his darkest moments, Alan was sensitive to the divine comedy that governs us all, and while we laughed, he strengthened. With each year, he became more and more like his father—not only in looks but in temperament, He was gentler than Davie.

He saw the world from a distant clime and was more cynical than his father. His humor captured the superficiality and nonsense he observed in ordinary life. If he leaned toward the cynical, it was only because he was acutely aware of the dichotomies that existed in our own family. He knew Davie adored Beck, but this did not prevent the repeated fun Davie made of her weight or her lack of knowledge—she read little, cared casually about politics, and believed her home was her castle.

But he loved her kindness, her softness, her beauty. All his life, Alan resented the fact that Beck was always the object of Davie's humor. In later years, Alan confessed that he "hated" Davie for belittling the mother he loved. The irony rested on the fact that Alan's humor too frequently turned on the foibles, weaknesses and pretensions of his siblings. His sense of their insecurities was astonishingly sharp and it was inevitable that it made its way into his parodies!

I would be remiss if I glossed over Alan's most significant value—friendship. Surely, many of us have had a friend we cherish, a friend who knew our inner selves, our complexities, our faults, our successes as well as our failures. But for Alan, his friends defined him. They were not simply those who agreed with him, or were as ambitious as he was, or followed his life after he left New York.

There was something almost inexplicable in his relationship with Robbie or Roy or Steve....They were a living part of him years later in his career in Atlanta. There was an inner security that each would always be there for the other.

Alan never explained his profound love for his friends, but we knew that, in every sense, they were brothers. Different from blood brothers, they never took each other for granted but cherished the gifts of what Italiani call *anima e cuore*! Such was this rare relationship in Alan's life. Each of his friends marched to a different drummer, yet my family was always aware that some indescribable bond united them in a way that had no language, that had no test, that had merely the memories of youth.

Chapter III

Funny Man

I couldn't say Alan was a "comedian"—he never told jokes, rarely laughed, and almost always put his thoughts on paper. Often it is difficult to "record" his writing without knowing the circumstances that caught his pen or the people he mercilessly castigated. Yet, there was much good humor when his subjects were those he loved—and forgave for their small lapses.

Reviewing his own parody of Longfellow's Hiawatha, Alan commented:

The "Song of HiRebecca" is indeed a triumphant return to the wellspring of American poetry: the experience of those courageous and bold folk heroes who traversed the Atlantic in search of a new game (Mahjongg, Canasta, et. al.) to replace the stultifying pastime of pinochle.. The saga, sung by a restrained yet moving persona is nevertheless a complex and multi-dimensional correlative of an existential "Search for the Self" by the archetypal heroine. Interestingly, the form of the verse complements perfectly the selected theme. The assonance, consonance, alliteration, and incremental repetition reveal that Tropfellow has learned his lesson well at the feet of Pound, Eliot, Roethke, and, of course, Longfellow. He concludes:. "But, as Eliot taught us, great poetry was not meant to be analyzed: What matters, Eliot preached, but never practiced, "is the whole poem."

In another capricious mood, Alan wrote a lengthy response to a book I had published on the poetry of Denise Levertov, Alan wrote:

> *The key to Rodgers' brilliant analysis of Levertov's work clearly appears in the first 237 pages of her new book. Rodgers finally lays to rest any doubt that the poet's earlier works preceded her later ones.... We learn that early in her career, Levertov had a reputation as a fine lyric poet. Later, when*

she emerged as a political dissident during the Vietnam War, her works were imbued with a strong social consciousness (which I might add, was more appropriate since words like 'love' and 'flower' don't count for much when a Vietcong is trying to shove a bayonet up your ass!).... Finally, as we have previously seen in Rodgers' earlier works on Eliot and Williams, we find a critical unity of rational analysis and poignant empathy, which leads this reviewer to a state of mind only experienced when reading a book written by an English professor—and which has been reproduced in volunteer subjects which have endured seventy-two hours of sensory isolation, ingested 250 milligrams of sodium pentathol, and then inhaled deeply over eight minutes from the tailpipe of a 1976 Buick.

Needless to say, Alan had never read the works of Eliot, Williams, or Levertov.

When not posing as a "literary critic" Alan found rich material in countless everyday life. In a frivolous moment, he sent the following to a friend:

> *Dear -------,*
>
> *I am writing to invite you to a "surprise" party to be given for me by my wife. I hasten to add that under no circumstances are gifts to be given (if you believe this then you also believe that Mrs. Arafat keeps a kosher kitchen...)...*

Since Alan took great delight at my becoming an English professor, he knew I would enjoy the following:

Dear Audrey,

Thanks to you for sending to my boys the books for which they could learn from for English writing of book reports correct. We want to really appreciate it as it don't cost us anything....We will work hardon them boy's so they can be the sucseses like we are. Some times we get disappointed because we don't know from wear they pick up such habets.

Love,

Your brother and fellow relative.

He loved us all, but was unable to resist poking fun at out postures, our "literary" assumptions, our inability to laugh at our pretensions until the moment a hand-written letter arrived from Alan reminding us of our foibles, our humility, our ego. We enjoyed minor successes, jolted by Alan's humorous reminders that, after all, we were not Longfellow or Levertov or T.S. Eliot! Did we forgive him? Our laughter speaks for itself!

Chapter IV

Becoming A Physician

Alan was no longer a "child"; he was no longer the family 'pet'; he was no longer the precocious favored wunderkind we all took half-seriously. For the next few years, he would be a dedicated medical student with little social life or family get-togethers. He moved into an apartment near Bellevue and we saw him on brief visits.

Before his acceptance into the Medical School, he had done superbly at New York University which enjoyed close ties to Bellevue. Davie urged him to "use his influence" since admission was difficult to receive, but Alan was adamant. He insisted that he make it on his own and he was successful! We were abashed for having so little faith in him when we well knew his excellent academic record. Still. Bellevue was a difficult mountain to climb, and Alan knew little else for the four years he attended his new profession. His reward came when he wrote the traditional show at graduation and was dragged on stage to receive a thundering applause. His father, dying of cancer, sat with his mother in the first row—awash with pride!.

This turning point in his life conjures up a kaleidoscope of images from the past—Alan as a tousled-headed baby, Alan writing satires on vulnerable family members, Alan more like Davie with each year…literate, complex, vibrating between humor and depression, moving from "boy" to "man". We knew him; yet there was a well of moods and desires that were beyond us.

These were lonely years for Alan. He had chosen a Residency in Psychiatry, not only because this field of medicine attracted him, but to better know himself. Though Davie was disappointed, devoted as he was to traditional medicine, Alan found Psychiatry gratifying and fascinating. And during this intensive period of training, he fell in love!

Patty Becker came into Alan's life during his Internship on a warm sunny day in October. Having met through friends, Patty visited Alan at the hospital on his "break" armed with a bagel and cream cheese, a captivating smile, and shining brown eyes. Thus was the beginning of their romance. They told no one of these visits until the end of Alan's Internship and well on his way to his Residency.

It would be difficult to explain what life was like for an aspiring Jewish medical student in New York during the 1940's. In most cases the student came from an immigrant Jewish family—dreaming of the magical future their children would have. Translated, this meant becoming a doctor or a lawyer with all the prestige these careers suggested. Becoming a doctor for the student meant arduous work, little social life, late hours studying, and virtually no failure! One's life was to make the parents proud. So success was the only option! Small wonder that the medical student of the '40's was socially inept, had little money for dating, and, in fact, knew few girls to date.

Seeing Patty's slender figure, chiseled face, and smiling encouragement, Alan was fated to capitulate. Hand in hand, enriched with bagel and cream cheese, the lovers planned their future. Alan had found in Patty a quiet, beautiful, adoring woman and moved further away from his close family ties. Patty Becker could not have been a more different person from the girls we knew. We laughed when a year earlier he told his Mother, "I want someone just like my sisters."

When his Internship was completed, they were married. Needless to say, Alan's parents were sorely disappointed. They had fantasized that their son would, one day, marry the daughter of rich parents who could help set him up in practice and open the door to a distinguished career. Nonetheless, they made a small wedding and wished them well.

Patty, hurt by the slight, never forgave them while Alan—madly in love—knew only of his happiness.

Chapter V

Patty

She was young, delicately lovely, soft-spoken, and innocent. In an earlier age one would call her "sweet." But they would not know this wisp of a girl or the depth of her dreams.

Patty knew little of the world outside the Bronx, but she knew the life she yearned for and that life began with Alan. Quietly but deeply, she returned the love he so eagerly held out to her.

To the Tropauers, Patty was an enigma. She had few friends while our house was constantly teeming with college mates, music, snacks, laughter and dancing to the small "music box" resounding loudly with the pop tunes of the day. Patty spoke little while we talked too much! She didn't seem interested in politics or learning a foreign language when Elinor and I were studying French, and she only became animated when Alan entered the room. Patty had no faults and slowly Elinor and I began to understand and like her. Yet, it became clear that no close tie was possible between Patty and our family, and the cool behavior of our parents only made the notion of a "growing friendship" untenable. Patty remained distant until her tragic death years later…

Soon after completing his Residency in Child Psychiatry, Alan and Patty toured the country in search of a city to begin his practice. Through former fellow-classmates at Bellevue and advice from Davie's friends and Alan's professors, the task was almost insurmountable!

They learned only that New York was impossible—living costs were high, familial relations were at best, polite, and Alan was ready for a new life while Patty quivered at the thought of leaving the only city she knew.

While California was tempting, Patty was adamant about locating as far from her mother and the simple routines she knew.

When they finally settled on Cincinnati, Patty knew she would never go home again. Cincinnati was an unlikely choice but highly recommended as having a bright future This mid-Western city posed a challenge to Alan in his first venture in medicine. That Cincinnati lacked the sophistication of New York or Boston posed no threat to Alan who sensed he was embarking upon a voyage in his brave new world. In truth, Cincinnati proved to be a highly successful venture—Alan made a rapid impression on his fellow physicians, and all would have been well except Patty felt lost in an atmosphere both uninteresting and cold. They made few friends and felt a sense of isolation.

As Alan gained in professional confidence and financial security, he began to investigate a city with a warmer climate and a more hospitable environment. Through the advice of fellow physicians, they settled on Atlanta.

As we know, all great cities have a distinct personality that sets them apart from other places. Paris, New York, San Francisco, New Orleans— each has qualities that contribute to their beauty and their ambiance. The city shapes the people there and conversely the people shape the city. Such is Atlanta where Alan chose to make his home and which formed the setting for his life of tears and laughter.

Atlanta was a newly discovered planet for Alan and Patty, who knew only New York and the boundaries of the Bronx. Although the *ignorante* thought of it as **THE South**—musing only on the Civil War, Atlanta is a harmonious compromise between distinctly "Southern" qualities and the modernity and progressiveness of its great northern neighbors.

Every great city is unique—and Atlanta's quality is that this bright star of Georgia balances with equal grace the flavor of the past: beauty, lush landscapes, and leisurely living with the spirit, complexity and ingenuity of modern metropolis.

Atlanta resonates greatly with the Civil War, and the suffering it ensued as the defeated. No work of art reminds us as the testimony of Margaret Mitchell's *Gone With The Wind* and the ever-present echoes of Martin Luther King's historic victories. They are the South's "Past"—

not long forgotten. And perhaps because of the seasonal heat and the ensuing slowing-down of activity Atlanta will often be thought of as a bucolic, relaxed environment. Added to the sense of "country-within-city," Atlanta's magnificent, enclosed private estates—close to the center of town—enhance the beauty of its boulevards. Atlanta is indeed a Green City.

Modern Atlanta lives harmoniously with its past. Amazingly, in the 20th century it has risen to become one of the busiest, richest, progressive American cities while still possessed of its "romantic" history. Today. Atlanta has little competition as one of the nation's proudest and most beautiful commercial and cultural centers. It is an artistic, industrial, and a transportation hub as well as a center for advanced medical research. As a manufacturer of chemicals, furniture, and textiles, the city is also the proud home of the Center for Disease Control and the corporate headquarters of several prestigious American business giants. Atlanta boasts the High Museum of Art as well as the Robert R. Woodruff Art Center. Frequent travelers are familiar with the

Hartsfield International Airport, one of the busiest in the United States. As a key center for up-to-date telecommunications, Insurance firms, and Sports arenas, this capital of Georgia has kept apace of America's future.

Thus, Atlanta—despite the echoes from its Southern history and the hint of y'all in its voice, this rich, charming, captivating city has succeeded in maintaining a balance between its historic Past and its vibrant Present. Both Patty and Alan immediately fell in love with the beauty and hospitality of Atlanta and looked forward to building a home for their "family." Patty prepared for their first child expected in a few short months—the first Southerner in our family!

Alan's practice flourished, and for the first time in their marriage, the "born and bred" New Yorkers happily adapted to the ambiance of Southern living though Patty was slow to make friends…

As the babies began to appear—three boys only two years apart—life in the Tropauer domain became busier and noisier. Jimmy, David, and Michael were robust, beautiful, and cheerful.

Outgoing as his nature was, Alan made friends throughout the medical community as he grew in stature with each passing year. He developed an interest in music, in challenging motion pictures, and he broadened his love for literature. His pleasure in Dickens or Tolstoy or Twain or Dostoyevsky transformed him from an intelligent, curious young doctor to a mature, complex, and introspective adult.

When Alan planned the construction of their home in Atlanta, every room contained built-in, ceiling to floor bookshelves. Unlike many doctors he knew, his interests ranged far beyond his professional commitment to Psychiatry. His taste in food was limited to Chinese fare...but Patty cared little for gourmet cooking.

While Alan was "growing" intellectually, Patty kept retreating into her own world! Her life centered on the house and the three boys. True, they were a twenty-four hour preoccupation, but Patty declined to hire anyone to help her. She assumed all of the responsibilities of the house. She refused a person to clean, did all her own cooking, catered to the demands small children are wont to make. She made few friends. Little by little, Patty—who was naturally reserved—retreated into the only world she knew, contented with her life and seemingly happy. To the family they viewed her as cold, but Patty never opened the door to intimacy and rarely spoke of Alan's family. Undaunted, we made periodic trips to Atlanta, driven by our love for Alan and our affection for his captivating children.

Looking back, it was not for us to judge Patty, but we were intrinsically a sharing family—our hearts, indeed, on our sleeves—and she was impenetrable for us. If Alan ever became disillusioned in his marriage as they appeared to follow separate paths, he never acknowledged it. Instead, he seemed to be more cynical, more reflective, more focused on his sons' growth Nor did Alan make jokes at Patty's expense!

Life in Atlanta seemed to be a model for the typical American family—the boys were "growing up" as we say; Alan's practice was doing well; the house they had built was handsome and comfortable....Then tragedy struck! After an early visit to Atlanta, Alan drove me to the airport and mentioned, quietly, that he was worried about Patty. She had developed a lump in her breast and her physician had advised her, "Let's watch it for a year."

I was horrified and Alan was visibly shaken. We both agreed that Patty needed attention immediately. But it was too late. Despite all medical attention, Patty suffered for more than a year from cancer that slowly robbed her of her life.

Alan was distraught, turning to all his medical colleagues for a magical means for Patty's recovery—to no avail. Patty, typically, never complained but used her rare moments free from pain to help the boys with their schoolwork and tried to follow a normal routine. Elinor and I visited whenever Alan told us Patty was in a brief remission, but she grew more ill as the cancer spread with a life of its own.

On a bleak windswept day, Alan laid Patty to rest. She wanted to be near her father and so she was that November in New York. Her sons—Jimmy (age 12), David (age 10), and Michael (age 8)—

each holding a white rose to place on the polished wooden casket—stood in stunned silence as the Rabbi intoned the sacred prayer for the departed.

Patty's sons were transfixed, as though not completely understanding why they were there and why the Rabbi was praying. I wept for Patty and for the life she did not have. She tasted so little of the world and was satisfied with crumbs of joy and the love of her small family. Alan held my hand—we needed no words to express our grief.

Chapter VI

The Children's Hour

This was the time when Alan turned to his three sons who waited for him to bring peace and solace and loving care after the trauma of losing their mother. Alan had little time for mourning as innocent faces sought comfort and solidity from the father who could scarcely sustain his own grief. The burden was enormous. No family was present to ease the overwhelming job of caregiver, meal planner, homework helper and the much needed presence of affection and hope. Alan alone gave them love, respect, a sympathetic ear, and the reassurance that he would always be there for them. These four years were, indeed, the children's hour.

As I muse about those lonely years and the overwhelming toll they exacted from Alan, I am haunted by Longfellow's moving poem when he touches on his own moment and the love for his children.

Between the dark and the daylight
When the night is beginning to lower,
Comes a pause in the day's occupation,
That is known as the Children's Hour.

I hear in the chamber above me
The patter of little feet,
The sound of a door that is opened.
And voices soft and sweet.

From my study I see in the lamplight,
Descending the broad hall stair,
Grave Alice and laughing Allegra,
And Edith with golden hair.

A whisper, and then a silence:
Yet I know by their merry eyes
They are plotting and planning together
To take me by surprise.

A sudden rush from the stairway,
A sudden raid from the hall!
By three doors left unguarded
They enter my castle wall!

They climb up into my turret
O'er the arms and back of my chair;
If I try to escape, they surround me;
They seem to be everywhere.

They almost devour me with kisses,
Their arms about me entwine
Till I think of the Bishop of Bingen
In his Mouse Tower on the Rhine!

Do you think O you blue-eyed banditi,
Because you have scaled the wall.
Such an old mustache as I am
Is not a match for you all.

I have you fast in my fortress
And will not let you depart,
But put you down into my dungeon
In the round-tower of my heart.

And there will I keep you forever,
Yes, forever and a day,
Till the walls shall crumble to ruin,
And moulder in dust away.

As the poet sets his playful children against his own certain death, the poignancy of his love is more intensified—the beauty more palpably real. And so for us all! Alan's closeness and affection for his boys remained in the "round-tower" of his heart—even as his responsibility for them grew.

Memory is capricious. A moment or two flash upon our inner consciousness—unannounced, broken bits of "happenings," poignant or joyful. But fragmentary as they are, memories link us to our past, reminding us that we did survive. Alan recalled those random echoes from the past even as he planned the future of his sons. They would go to college, choose a profession, marry, and raise their own families. And so they did. The boys, heartened by both their youth and Alan's optimism drove themselves to succeed.

The house—too large for Alan and the boys— remained the center of life though the mother who cherished it was no longer its keeper. Alan had always loved the great, expansive rooms, the delicately nurtured flower beds that wound round the structure, the tall, slim trees that shuttered out the summer heat. He would never give it up. Prophetically, he would die in it. For Alan the house was all he'd really wanted materially, come loss or catastrophe. It was truly a male domain. Teenage friends wrestled on the sweet-smelling turf. Alan, when free, usually could be found stretched out on his bed, reading Melville and Twain, Tolstoy and Fitzgerald. These were his moments of peace— hidden away from the world of women—lacking the courage and the incentive to search out male companionship.

When we could, Elinor and I flew to Atlanta to offer companionship and comfort to Alan and to learn more about the boys—growing faster than we could imagine. More mature for their years, they were helpful in the house and pleasure for their father. They were tall and handsome and loving. On every visit I made, I was treated with affection, respect and love. Near or miles away that we were, they knew they had family that cared for them and were absorbed in their future. They were a true combination of Patty's sweetness and good looks and Alan's sense of humor and conviviality. Alan played his dual role as Father and Mother with humor and camaraderie whether it be football, basketball, or just plain wrestling. Despite his varied responsibilities and professional commitments, Alan was foremost a father.

Chapter VII

After Great Pain

No matter the loss, no matter the lingering pain and sadness, the strong recover. My father, Davie, often said: "This too shall pass," and in the moments after tragedy this is hard to believe. But most people discover they are stronger than they had ever imagined. It is memories; it is responsibilities—perhaps merely an indescribable will to keep living—that urges most victims of loss to seek a new life. Not to forget the past but invite the future.

How well Emily Dickinson knew this!

After great pain a formal feeling comes
The Nerves sit ceremonious like Tombs—
The stiff Heart questions was it He that bore,
And Yesterday or Centuries before?
The Feet, mechanical, go round,

Of Ground, or Air, or Ought—

A Wooden way

Regardless grown,

A Quartz contentment, like a stone—

This is the Hour of Lead—

Remembered, if outlived.

As freezing persons, recollect the Snow—

First Chill—then Stupor—then the letting

go—

And so Alan recovered—to recapture happiness, to recapture the joy that comes with a renewed love for people. The years passed quickly.

The three small boys grew, tall and straight and their "Southern" drawl added to their charm. They filled the house with their laughter, their camaraderie, their love and support of their father. Jimmy was the eldest—in looks strikingly like his father. Delicately built, he reminded one of Patty, but his tow-head and fair complexion were unmistakably Alan. Though slight and seemingly frail, Jimmy was strong, ambitious, and a formidable challenge for his brothers. He was articulate, warm and talkative, and—best of all—had a rye sense of humor that endeared him to all those who knew him. As the eldest, he was Alan's chief supporter and confidante. He chose engineering as his career and remained, to Alan's relief, in Atlanta after a few years in southern Georgia.

David, named for his grandfather. was Patty's child—his dark eyes and handsome stature recalled the young mother whom they all brought to life in their random memories. David was "success" from childhood. In his teens, David was fun-loving, warm, talkative, and social. As he matured, he became more serious and soft spoken. He worked hard, hewed to his desire to become an important link in the business arena, and embraced the world that his mother had rejected. Of all the Tropauer boys, he was the strongest, the most mature, the most speculative. He was generally quiet, but David had goals that, in time, he would achieve with stunning success.

If every family had to have a "scamp," it could not find a more loving than Alan's youngest son. Michael was a success story without effort. Perhaps because he was so young when he lost his mother, Michael defies deep analysis. In looks, he was his father's son with a personality that recalled the sweetness and childlike nature of Patty. Michael, though, was a winner—popular with the world at large and warm and lovable in his family. Mike's sense of humor was surely a glance backward at his father whose love for this youngest son could not be measured. His easy-going charm would change in the years that followed with more responsibility. During his teens. he was content to be the "kid" who pleased with his smile and affability. He always provided fun and affection to the Atlanta atmosphere. All this would change when he met and married Debbie When his wife gave birth to triplets, he left "childhood" behind. Without much effort, Michael enjoyed the success that Jimmy and David worked so hard to achieve.

Alan, busy with his practice, had no time— or perhaps no will—for a life "outside." All his free time was spent with his sons; his few friends constantly attempted to interest him in the eligible Southern ' beauties' of Atlanta but to no avail. Yet, giving in to their entreaties, he dated several times, never finding the "right" person, or perhaps not by searching! He complained often to me "They are all so ambitious sophisticated, and smart." He laughed, "They scare me with their brains and beauty."

In fact, Alan was not ready or anxious to meet the woman who could fulfill his life. And then, unexpectedly, Eileen "happened." There are times in our lives when we make plans and the plans go awry, and there are other times when we are caught by surprise, when what we never could have forecast occurs and our lives are changed dramatically. In Alan's life, at the age of 55. it was Eileen.

I first met Eileen Ruzann when a summer program for high school students in need of academic proficiency was initiated at Penn State University. Eileen taught during the school year at the prestigious Abington School in Philadelphia, and her great gift for communicating with young people was phenomenal. Students took daily courses in several subjects and Eileen worked with me on the English program. We soon became warm friends and my admiration for her increased as I sat in her classroom and watched this young teacher hold a class of youngsters transfixed. After years of teaching, I cannot recall a room filled with restless students respond so quickly and eagerly to a charismatic, engaged teacher who clearly loved her calling.

Vivacious is only one quality that comes to mind in describing Eileen. Whether reciting a prose passage from Hemingway or reading a poem by Robert Frost. Eileen's large green eyes and lilting voice combined with her sensitivity to language.

Mere words on a page were transformed into a magical experience for students who had never heard poetry read aloud. I recognized Eileen's gift instantly and I urged her to further graduate work and the joy of teaching literature beyond the high school level. And so, Eileen joined the graduate body at Penn State and we would remain friends forever. The work was difficult, but Eileen succeeded in earning her Master's Degree in a short time.

The years pass quickly and it became difficult for us to maintain our friendship since Eileen married, moved to Florida and gave birth to twin boys. Yet we always kept in touch as she moved through divorce, re-marriage and divorce again. All during this period, despite being a single mother of twins, Eileen kept teaching. She heard the news in my family from our frequent visits and telephone conversations since both of us were determined to sustain our closeness.

Many years before, when Eileen was studying at Penn State, Alan and Eileen had a brief encounter. They liked each other, laughed a great deal, but the time was not auspicious for a deepening relationship. Eileen was to marry a music teacher from Abington, and Alan was absorbed by his studies in medicine. Time and space precluded more than a fleeting yet promising "friendship." In spite of all, Eileen kept track of Alan's life. She knew Alan's Patty had died and of Alan's loneliness. True, they had met for one brief moment, but now—older, wiser, and free—they were to reach out for one another....A random call from Eileen changed both her life and Alan's.

"I'm coming North with the boys and we have a three-hour wait in Atlanta. Do you think Alan would come to meet me?"

Alan agreed instantly but asked,

"How will I know her?"

Eileen's reply.

"I'll have a twin on either arm."

As Eileen's flight de-planed, Alan stood nervously in the back of the Reception Area studying the faces of weary passengers off to distant destinations. Then Eileen appeared, her eyes searching the crowd meeting friends and relatives. Tentatively, she approached an old man and asked, "Alan?" The man smiled and shook his head—clearly disappointed. Alan watched and laughingly came forward. Without an awkward moment, the boys, now fifteen, were shuttled off to inspect Atlanta's airport, while Eileen and Alan drank Cokes in the airport bar. For three hours they talked and fell in love. Eileen glowed and Alan knew in his heart that he had met the woman he searched for. She was forty. He was fifty-five.

These were the halcyon years for Eileen and Alan. After a whirlwind "courtship" that included countless flights between Miami and Atlanta, two middle-aged lovers joined hands in holy matrimony. The bride wore pristine white and the Rabbi opened his remarks—not with a prayer—but the observation:

Ladies and Gentlemen, we would not be here if it were not for Audrey.

Alan's boys welcomed a female presence in the house after years of pizza, Chinese, and "Lean Cuisine". They loved her cheeriness, her interest in their lives, their little jokes and stories. She knew their interests for she had boys of her own—she listened to them and was always sympathetic to their needs. The kitchen became the central hang-out when Eileen was there. The twins, Jason and Aaron, effortlessly became a part of the household and genuinely looked up to their new brothers. Eileen breathed new life into the neglected yet still beautiful house, lifting the pall that had hovered over it since Patty's death. With her skill, she brought her fresher, happier spirit. She transformed every room with delicate china, with objects of art, with new furniture where wear had left its mark, with priceless carpets and silk curtains. An aura of light gradually replaced the tired, mourning building. The boys, touched by her enthusiasm, joined in her efforts to bring love and beauty into the home Alan had always dreamed of.

But foremost, the relationship between Alan and Eileen shaped the serenity and happiness of this new family. In the covering blessing of darkness, the passion of their love was transformed with tears and laughter. Miraculously, they had found each other before age and infirmity had made their inroads. Life quickened as each day they discovered another interest, another quality, another dream in the other. Were they different? Alan was ever the cynic, Eileen the optimist. Eileen followed her religious upbringing without question; Alan was the eternal skeptic. Eileen loved to travel; Alan chose to stay at home with a good book. But both filled their leisure hours with music, great books, the movies, and good food. Here the definition varied. Alan was a devotee of Chinese restaurants while Eileen spent days concocting Jewish dishes for armies of friends. Needless to say, Alan never contested her choice, but he was seen frequently at one Chinese emporium or another.

It was primarily Eileen who opened the physical world for Alan. Together with their five children, they took an extended trip to Israel where Alan, excitedly, sensed the palpable reality of being a Jew. Like many New York Jews, he "observed" the holy days, but had never felt the passion and intensity of struggling Israel. In infinite ways he was touched by what he saw. They travelled regularly, tasting new foods, hearing new languages, experiencing new, beautiful landscapes. This was not Patty's world— it was Eileen's—offered to Alan with loving arms.

As the boys grew older, each married and created new Tropauers. The house rang with the laughter of young children, their antics, their refreshing energy.

Both Eileen and Alan fiercely defended each other's shortcomings. They laughed away insignificant differences. Above all, they never forgot the unhappiness of the past and filled each day with silent gratitude. For twenty years, despite the routine quality of ordinary living, their deep affection sustained them. Their love endured.

Chapter VIII

The Last Hurrah

For twenty years they lived and loved—two middle-aged people with the vitality and optimism that had brought them together. For twenty years They worked, travelled and let the new world in. For twenty years They savored their togetherness after the long, lonely four. There was much to

be thankful for, much to dream of, and much to endure. They followed each other's careers—Eileen teaching English to college-bound youngsters, Alan again deeply absorbed in his practice of Child Psychiatry. Psychiatry. They nurtured five sons to manhood endowed with promise hey nurtured five sons to manhood endowed with promise and stability. For twenty years they came to know each other's moods, inner hopes and fantasies, fears and quirks, and the depth and breadth of the love they never took for granted.

Only Eileen can recall the substance of the sometime hectic life they lived during those years. Today, Alan is gone, and Pennsylvania was countless miles away from Georgia and the day-to-day happenings Eileen and Alan experienced. Yet the calls were frequent and the visits as often as possible with our busy schedules.

The Atlanta house buzzed with activity. Eileen was a party girl—nothing pleased her more than a houseful of friends and relatives. Birthdays, anniversaries, and countless major or minor Jewish holidays called for a party. Because she loved to cook, to lavishly serve up all manner of delicacies, Eileen thrived on this carnival of celebrations. For the first time since Patty's death, Alan enjoyed the parties and warmed to the new friendships they brought. But there were also the quiet times when they both watched movies, went to concerts, or curled up with a book. They shared—in these tranquil moments—their deepest thoughts, their fears, their happiness.

But there was another part of their lives—for Alan, the entire universe beyond Atlanta opened up. Their travel experiences alternated regularly with home activities. Eileen recalls the many trips they took both abroad and in the regions of the States new to both of them.

Among the many countries they would explore were Eileen's favorite haunts in Europe and the Western United States. For Alan, it was all new, exciting—each country offering sights and sounds he could never imagine had Eileen not opened the door to other worlds.

It would be impossible to envision the enormity of these new experiences on Alan. No longer was his life circumscribed by three young boys, the practice of psychiatry and the environs of Atlanta—fascinating as that city may have been. Earth opened its arms to a neophyte and he embraced it with love and enthusiasm.

Thus, over the twenty years of their marriage, travel was their favorite diversion. The boys were independent—married with families of their own. Jimmy became an engineer, but after the tragic death of his young wife, found a new life with Vickie and the love of two tousled-headed children—the mirror image of their father. David made rapid strides in the world of hospital administration in and enlarged the family circle with two dark-eyed children. Only years later did David lose Ryan, a mere sixteen years old, in a horrendous accident that cast a pall over his charmed success.

Every tragedy we experience brings back almost unforgettable events wrenched from the past. I recall writer William Faulkner's words: "Memory believes before knowing remembers" and memory haunts forever my earliest experience with death.

I was only ten and my closest friend was Mimi—a 19th century vision of beauty—delicate, soft-spoken, loving. We were inseparable—playing children's games, sharing secrets, laughing. Then, one terrible day, I was brought to Mimi's bedside where she reached up and took my hand. Her slight form lay still on the white sheet. Though wan and speechless, she smiled faintly. Her eyes seemed to say what her lips could not express. Holding my hand, Mimi died. I recall only disbelief and confusion and Mimi's hand in mine. But that faint image of her smile will be with me until I die. Not understanding, feeling only confusion and disbelief memory haunts forever my earliest experience with death—this was my first encounter with death. These memories come rushing back when I think of the death of David's Ryan and the bitter tears inevitably follow. Yet, better days were promised me.

These would be Eileen's and Alan's golden years. They were free of parental obligations, free of economical burdens, though hardly rich, and physically fit to wander the exotic corners of the earth.

At first, they favored cruises as travel neophytes to European ports: stopping along the Western Mediterranean and—on another cruise—the

Eastern Mediterranean. They were ready to explore land tours in European and more exotic historical areas: Poland and Budapest and Prague. Alan, long interested in his family origins, discovered that the town of Tropau had undergone the name change to Opava—today a part of Poland. They walked the tragic steps of six million Jews who died in concentration camps and wept bitter tears as they reconstructed that horrendous chapter of human infamy.

But by far, the most frightening experience in their travels occurred during the now infamous 9/11 massacre. Eileen and Alan were on a cruise when their ship stopped perilously close to Egyptian waters at the exact time that bombers attacked the two lofty towers of the Trade Center. They listened to radio accounts of the scores of innocent people hurled to their deaths. Incredibly hundreds of miles away, the 9/11 disaster was felt by the travelers of the cruise ship—among them Eileen and Alan. Only Eileen can describe the hysteria and chaos among the travelers who expected momentarily an attack from the Egyptian mainland. Hours after the first plane hurled itself at the Trade Center, the gay, shipboard revelers were transformed into a crouching, shocked mob—shivering, hiding, weeping, almost mindless mass. Death faced them at any moment, and if not for the quick thinking of the courageous Captain, the life of the cruise ship could well have been fatal.

Eileen and Alan kept cool heads and fervent prayers in this crisis and managed to transcend the danger by thinking little and struggling to pacify terrorized passengers—though their hearts were beating loudly. Their lives hung upon moments, but they survived. Their cruise ship escaped perhaps because the World's eyes were on the two graceful Towers falling to their fiery demise.

Needless to say, Eileen and Alan confined their future travels to land tours. They swam in Florida's warm waters, lounged in the comfort of the Blue Ridge Mountains, and luxuriated in the intoxicating beauty of the Bahamas....Their experience on the cruise ship the day of 9/11 haunted them periodically, but they never lost their love for the exotica of travel. Most of their travelling consisted of visits to family, old haunts, remembered friends and, of course, their treasured

New York. Their nearly twenty years were active, interesting, and memorable, and their love for each other held it all together.

Chapter IX

Alan and Audrey

I would be amiss if I neglected to consider the lifelong relationship between Alan and me that differed from that between most siblings. The ten year gap in our ages produced enormous differences that only time could obliterate and even then we were almost a generation apart.

Siblings, contrary to the myths abounding them, have a complex relationship that defies simplification. Close and loving all of our lives, Alan, and I were in constant intermittent conflict due, no doubt, to differing values, alternate lifestyles and inherent qualities. To most people, sisters and brothers shared similar personalities—and likes and dislikes—owing to identical nurturing, identical environment and agreeable wills.

Nothing could be further from the "clichés" than the enigmatic relationship of Alan and me. Often, we seemed embroiled in a battle while above all else we were loving, honest, and strongly defensive when the other was "attacked."

Both cultivated lifelong friendships and cherished family ties. Each held the highest standards for the other, which accounted for their numerous arguments and numerous reconciliations. Above all, they knew each well and weathered disagreements with humor. In the end, they respected, took pride in their sibling, and emphasized their loyalty with love.

I was an extrovert and acted largely by instinct while Alan preferred the workings of the mind which, no doubt, led him to the profession of Psychiatry. Both of us were avid readers though Alan preferred Tolstoy. Dostoyevsky, and Solgenitzkin while I read and re-read Hemingway, Faulkner and F. Scott Fitzgerald. I treasured expensive clothes, but Alan paid scant attention, all his life, to the outward show of material wealth, a few exceptions aside.

Both respected, took pride in, and loved the other. No siblings were as combative, yet as close and understanding in their relationship in a complex world. They survived the tears and shared the laughter.

Chapter X

The Worldly Hope

Disaster creeps in on little cat feet. First a nondescript pain, easily ignored, then a persistent ache, then an unbearable, knife-edged blow to stop the breath. This was the progress of Alan's final

illness. So busy was he with taking trips, visiting relatives in the East, hosting their growing friendships, and the overwhelming occupation of fathering five growing sons that Alan—often careless of his own health—ignored the even-increasing ache in his body. Finally, able no longer to wash away the pain, Alan consulted with a fellow urologist. On a warm morning in the heart of Spring, he learned what he had long suspected but refused to admit. It was cancer.

Though the months dragged by, punctuated by increasing pain, activity seemed to fly by on silent wings. It became clear that surgery was mandatory as a step against metastasis—the dreaded word for carcinoma victims.

Alan fought like the knowledgeable physician he was. He weathered the surgery, using all the medical know-how, joking his way through, to keep Eileen and the boys calm and to soothe his own nerves. When he called me on the phone, he kept his tone clinical and analytical while I, frantically, tried to hold my own conversational voice.

These were horrendous weeks. Yet, after the effects of the surgery waned, Alan seemed his former self. True, such a surgery does give the patient brief—but thankful—relief. Alan and Eileen grasped at this momentary respite from what they knew was inevitable. To the surprise of their closest friends and relatives, they journeyed to State College to celebrate my 80th birthday. No one knew of his illness as he laughed and mingled with all our guests, not knowing that he carried below "the bag" a reminder that rarely left him.

The next venture was even more dangerous as well as exciting, but indicative of the courage of these two. Casting aside gloom and doom—only for the faint-hearted—they set sail on a cruise of Eastern Europe, there to forget the present and live only for the moment: the blue Mediterranean, the Mosques, the sylvan sky at dusk, the laughter of fellow voyagers. It was the last ray of hope and they cherished it with the blessing of enlightened awareness.

And suddenly, the spectre of death became the dreaded reality. Pain grew like a ragged weed as Alan fought each onslaught with drugs and sleep.

Days slipped into weeks as he became weaker—unable to eat, to walk, to open his eyes to the stunned family encircling him. Speech was too painful, gestures only to express the humblest desires. Reality merged with the random thoughts of the dying as he whispered the names of those he loved and grasped for—Elinor, Eileen, and Audie. Yes, even today his call: Audie, Audie echoes in my ears.

Good night, sweet Prince, I whisper back.

The Worldly Hope men set their Hearts upon

Turns Ashes—or it prospers and anon

Like snow upon the Desert's dusty Face

Lighting a little hour or two is gone.

The Worldly Hope men set their Hearts upon

Turns Ashes—or it prospers and anon

Like snow upon the Desert's dusty Face

Lighting a little hour or two is gone.